anythink

D0574799

At the Wheel

I Want to Drive an

Ambulance

Henry Abbot

illustrated by
Aurora Aguilera

PowerKiDS press.

New York

Published in 2017 by The Rosen Publishing Group, Inc.
29 East 21st Street, New York, NY 10010

First Edition

Managing Editor: Nathalie Beullens-Maoui
Editor: Theresa Morlock
Book Design: Michael Flynn
Illustrator: Aurora Aguilera

Library of Congress Cataloging-in-Publication Data

Names: Abbot, Henry, author.
Title: I want to drive an ambulance / Henry Abbot.
Description: New York : PowerKids Press, [2017] | Series: At the wheel |
  Includes index.
Identifiers: LCCN 2016027644| ISBN 9781499427622 (paperback book) | ISBN
  9781499426670 (6 pack) | ISBN 9781499429411 (library bound book)
Subjects: LCSH: Emergency medical technicians–Juvenile literature. |
  Ambulance drivers–Juvenile literature.
Classification: LCC RC86.5 .A23 2017 | DDC 616.02/5092–dc23
LC record available at https://lccn.loc.gov/2016027644

Manufactured in the United States of America

CPSIA Compliance Information: Batch #BW17PK: For Further Information contact Rosen Publishing, New York, New York at 1-800-237-9932

Contents

I want to drive an ambulance.

What would it be like?

Ambulances are really
important. They help
people who are sick
or hurt.

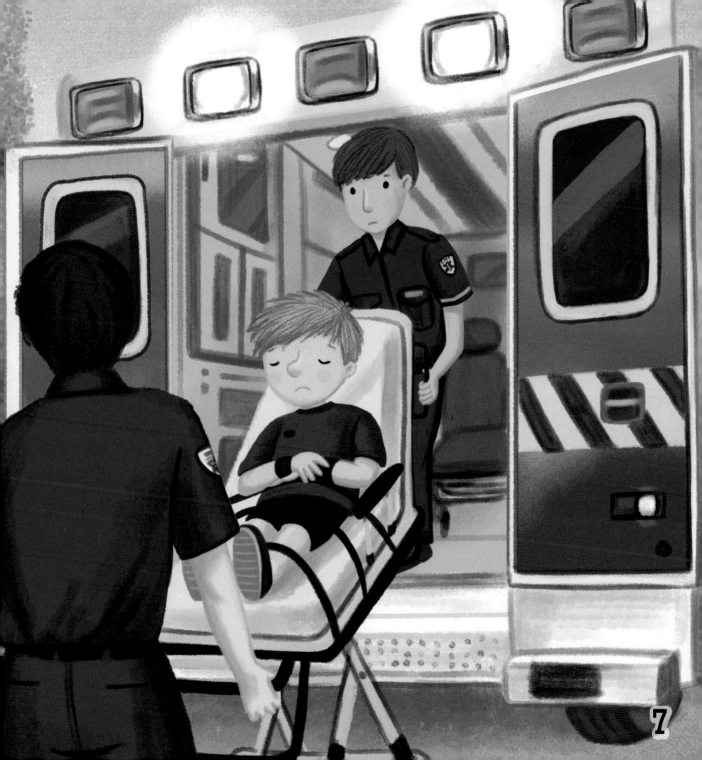

I'm an ambulance driver today.

I have a big job to do.

Someone calls and says they're hurt.

They need an ambulance.

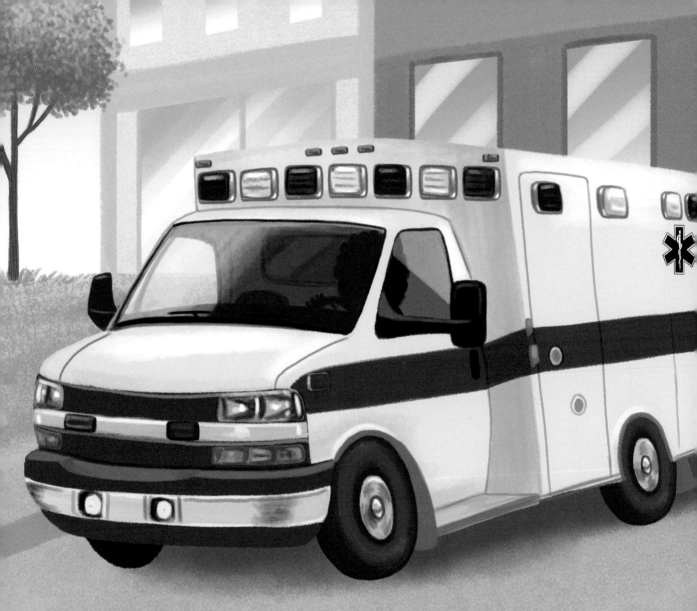

I make the ambulance go fast.

Time is important when
someone is hurt.

I press a button.

It turns on the lights and siren. The siren is loud!

The siren tells people an
ambulance is coming.

Other cars move out of the way.

The ambulance is here!

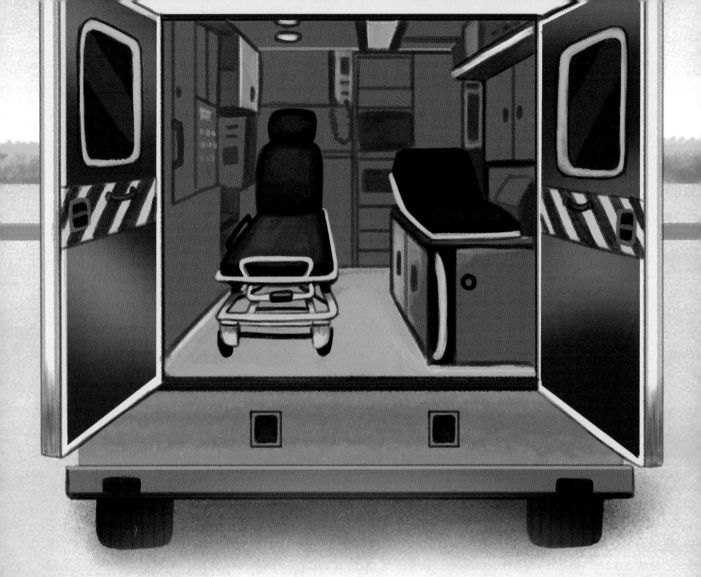

The back of an ambulance has tools
that make people feel better.

The ambulance is big enough to carry people to the hospital.

We're going there next.

I turn on the ambulance and it's time to go. We'll be at the hospital soon.

Words to Know

hospital

lights

siren

Index